The Lunch Thief

Anne C. Bromley   Illustrated by Robert Casilla

TILBURY HOUSE PUBLISHERS, GARDINER, MAINE

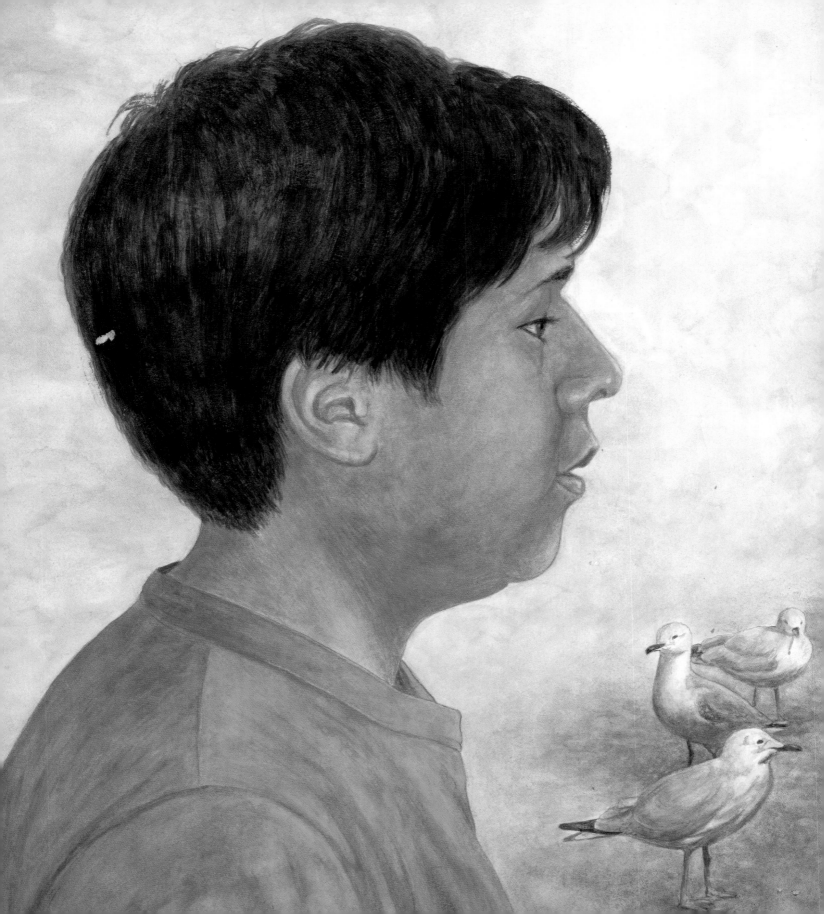

I'm so hungry I could eat the crumbs the seagulls left behind. They fly in from the coast every day to clean up the schoolyard after lunch. Mama usually packs me at least two burritos, a bag of corn chips, a carrot, and an apple. Once a week, she puts in a slice of her famous lemon poundcake.

"Hey, Rafael, how come you're not eating?" asks my best friend, Alfredo, as he's about to bite into a thick tuna-fish sandwich.

"I forgot my lunch," I lie.

"Ha! You never forget food," says Alfredo, poking my belly.

Eating is my second most favorite thing to do. My favorite thing is pitching for the Beckerville School baseball team.

Truth is, Kevin Kopeck, the new kid, stole my lunch. He took it during geography class when we were away from our desks. We were spread out on the floor, drawing maps of the seven continents on butcher paper. I saw him out of the corner of my eye when he pulled my lunch bag from underneath my desk and stuffed it into his backpack. When the lunch bell rang, he ran out of the room like greased lightning.

Right now, Kevin is sitting by himself next to the stone wall, eating my burrito!

I should report him, but he'll figure out who did it, and he'll probably pick a fight after school. He's tall and skinny, but he looks tough and fast—like maybe he could pack a mean punch. I may be big for my age, but I'm not a fighter. Mama says fighting is for cowards.

    When we're back in class after lunch, Kevin sits behind me.
He pokes me in the back. "Hey, doughboy, you got any candy
in your backpack?"
    "Cut it out!" I hiss back.
    "What's your name, anyway?" Kevin asks.
    "Rafael. Rafael Muñoz."
    "That's a funny name."
    "No funnier than yours."

"I'll give you a quarter for some candy." He reaches into his pocket.

"Is that all you've got?" I ask.

"For now," he says, in a whisper. His scraggly hair almost covers his eyes.

"I don't have any candy. I don't have any food because somebody stole my lunch."

I turn around when Mrs. Miller taps me on the shoulder. Kevin puts his head down on the desk.

"I think you boys better stop talking unless you want to spend an hour with me after school." Mrs. Miller writes our names on the whiteboard. First warning.

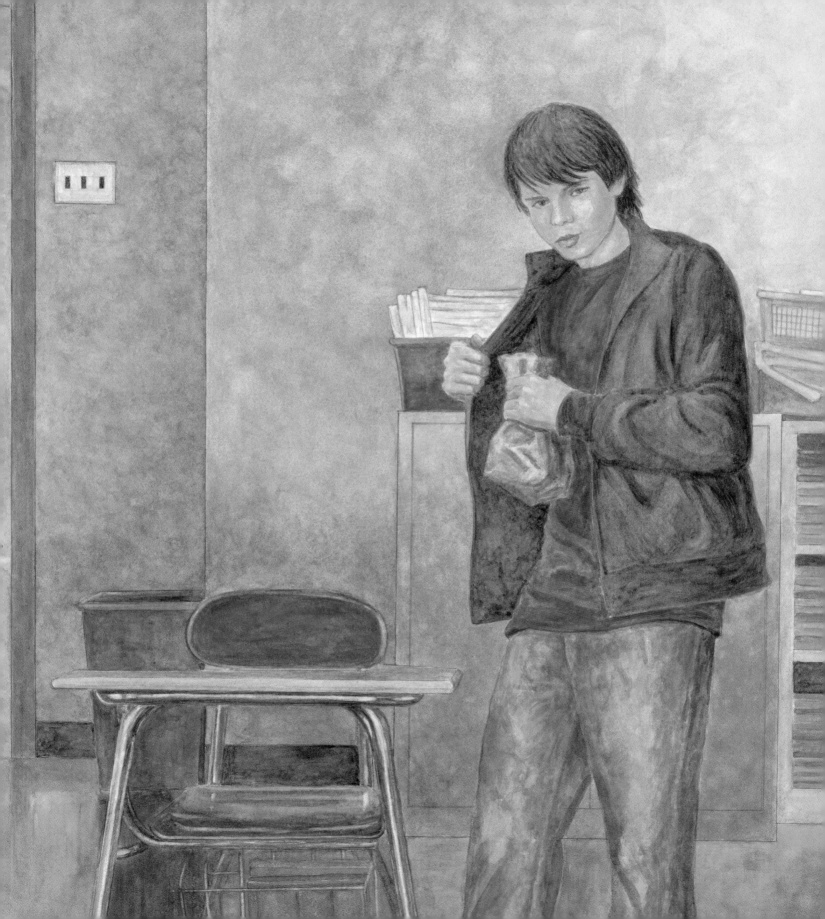

The next day Kevin steals Alfredo's lunch while Alfredo is in the restroom. Kevin grabs it from under Alfredo's desk and stuffs it into his jacket pocket. I shout, "Hey! What are you doing?"

Mrs. Miller scolds me for talking and writes my name on the board. Again. One more time and I get detention. If I get detention Mama will be mad at me because I've got to be home in time to baby-sit Lupita, my little sister, while Mama works her shift at the hospital.

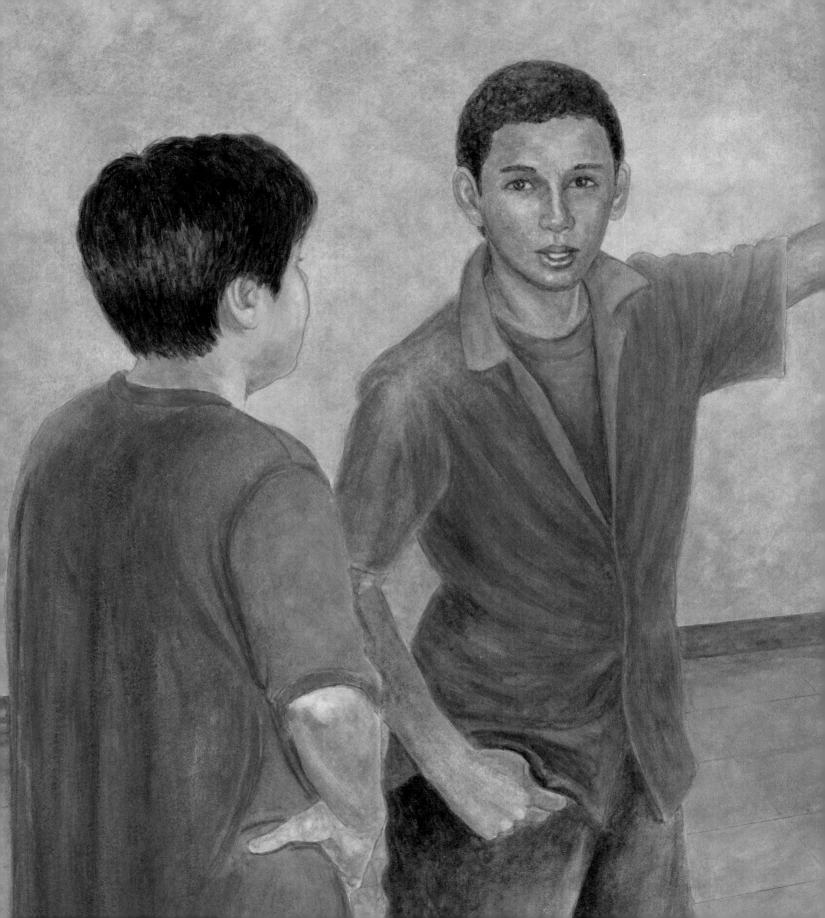

Alfredo and I look for Kevin along the stone wall, but he's not there. He's nowhere in the yard. When the bell rings after lunch, he runs out of the Media Center. He probably figured he'd be safe munching on Alfredo's lunch there.

Mama always says, "Use your mouth before your fists," so I give my mouth a chance the next day in social studies before the lunch bell.

"Hey, Kevin. What's up?" I ask.

"Nothing." He just stares ahead like I'm not there.

"Where are you from, anyway?" I ask.

"Jacinto Valley."

"Where the fires were last month?"

"Yeah. No big deal," he says, tossing the hair out of his eyes.

No big deal? Half of Jacinto Valley was burned down by wildfires that spread all over the county. Beckerville was lucky. The fires danced all around our town. There was so much smoke in the air we had to wear surgical masks when we went outside, but no one's house burned down.

Kevin doesn't want to talk about the fires.

"You got any candy? I've got a quarter." He's biting his nails.

"We're not allowed to eat before lunch," I say. I want to tell him to keep his mitts off my lunch bag, which is hidden deep down in my backpack, squished burritos and all. But I don't. A little voice tells me to shut up. Mama says it's a good idea to listen to that voice. Once in a while I do.

When the bell rings, Kevin bolts out of the classroom like a scared pony, and I hear Karen Olmsted scream, "Somebody stole my lunch!"

On Saturday, Mama, Lupita, and I go shopping for groceries. When Mama stops at the light before turning into the parking lot, it seems to stay red forever. So I look over at the Budget Motel, and there's this skinny kid with stringy hair walking toward one of the rooms. He's holding a bundle of laundry. When he turns to close the door behind him, I see that it's Kevin Kopeck.

"Do you know him?" Mama asks.

"Yeah, he's the new kid from Jacinto Valley," I say.

"He and his family are probably living in that motel room. A lot of people from Jacinto Valley lost their homes, lost everything in those fires." Mama turns the car into the shopping plaza. "He may be living there for a long time."

I think about my lunch. Every day Mama makes me two burritos. My baseball coach says I should lose some weight. Maybe I don't need two burritos.

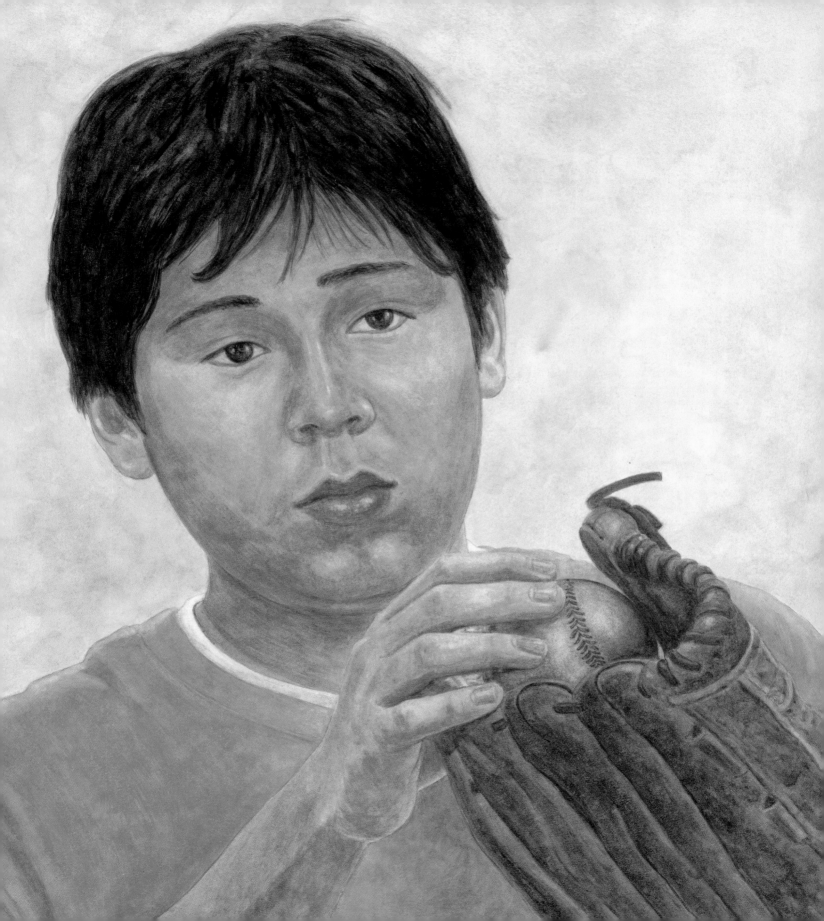

On Monday, Mrs. Miller puts us in different groups for a new project. Kevin Kopeck is in my group. Before we start talking about who's going to do what, I ask him if he'd like to hang out with Alfredo and me at lunch.

"Sure," he says.

"Do you like burritos?" I ask, handing him a full lunch bag, including a slice of lemon poundcake.

He shakes the hair out of his eyes, then smiles a little. "Yeah, I do. Thanks."

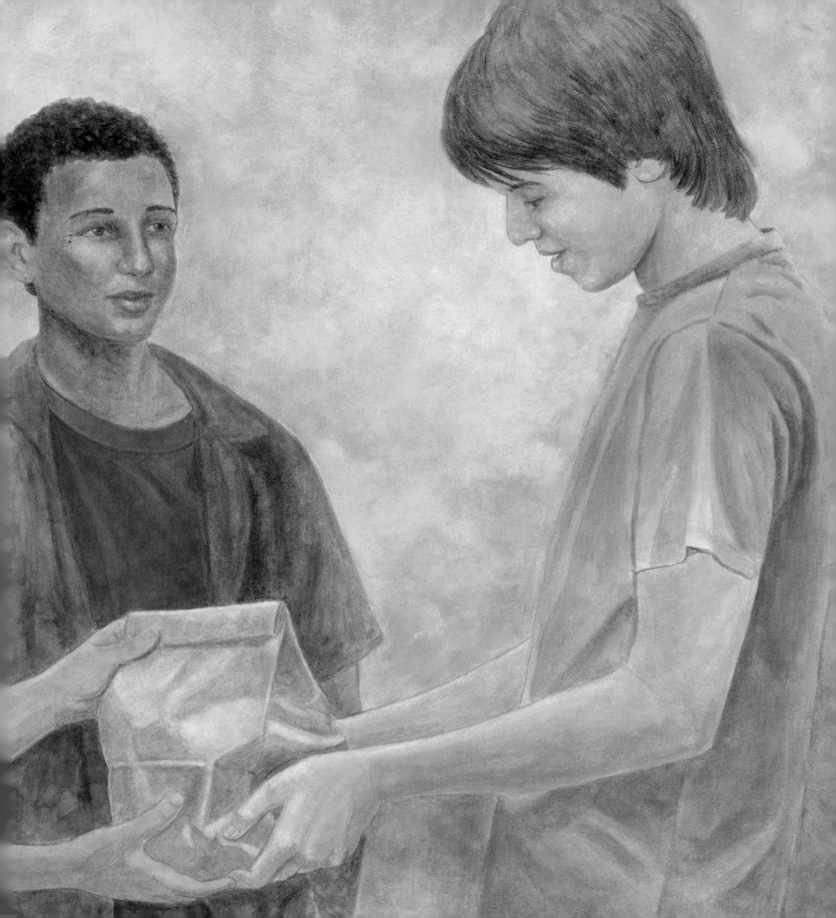

Then he reaches into his pocket and pulls out a quarter.
I just smile back.

TILBURY HOUSE, PUBLISHERS

103 Brunswick Avenue, Gardiner, Maine 04345

800–582–1899 • www.tilburyhouse.com

First hardcover edition: July 2010 • 10 9 8 7 6 5 4 3 2 1

To my husband Rod, who is always there to listen to my stories and suggest a better word or two or three. —A.B.

To my daughter Emily, who served as the model for Karen Olmsted in this book. —R.C.

Library of Congress Cataloging-in-Publication Data

Bromley, Anne C., 1950-

The lunch thief / Anne C. Bromley ; illustrated by Robert Casilla. — 1st hardcover ed.

  p. cm.

Summary: Rafael is angry that a new student is stealing lunches, but he takes time to learn what the real problem is before acting.

  ISBN 978-0-88448-311-3 (hardcover : alk. paper)

  [1. Stealing—Fiction. 2. Schools—Fiction. 3. Homelessness—Fiction. 4. Conduct of life—Fiction.]

  I. Casilla, Robert, ill. II. Title.

  PZ7.B7872Lun 2009

  [Fic]—dc22   2008045822

Designed by Geraldine Millham, Westport, Massachusetts.

Printed and bound by Sung In Printing Ltd., Dang Jung-Dong 242-2, GungPo-si, Kyunggi-do, Korea; April 2010.